JER Korte
Korte, Steven,
Metropolis monkey trouble /
$5.95
on1191241078

WITHDRAWN

W9-DJB-274

AMAZING ADVENTURES OF THE DC SUPER-PETS!™

Metropolis Monkey Trouble

by **Steve Korté**

illustrated by **Art Baltazar**

Superman created by Jerry Siegel and Joe Shuster by special arrangement with the Jerry Siegel Family

PICTURE WINDOW BOOKS
a capstone imprint

Published by Picture Window Books, an imprint of Capstone.
1710 Roe Crest Drive
North Mankato, Minnesota 56003
www.capstonepub.com

Copyright © 2021 DC Comics.
DC SUPER-PETS and all related characters and elements © & ™ DC Comics.
WB SHIELD: ™ & © Warner Bros. Entertainment Inc. (s21)

All rights reserved. No part of this publication may be reproduced in whole or
in part, or stored in a retrieval system, or transmitted in any form or by any
means, electronic, mechanical, photocopying, recording, or otherwise, without
written permission of the publisher.

Library of Congress Cataloging-in-Publication Data
Names: Korté, Steve, author. | Baltazar, Art, illustrator.
Title: Metropolis monkey trouble / by Steve Korté ; illustrated by Art Baltazar.
Description: North Mankato, Minnesota : Picture Window Books, an imprint
of Capstone, [2021] | Series: The amazing adventures of the DC super-pets
| Audience: Ages 5–7. | Audience: Grades K–1. | Summary: "A chunk of
Kryptonite has turned Superman into a wild animal! He's on the streets and
looking to make monkey trouble. Can Beppo the Super-Monkey stop him from
making Metropolis his playground?"—Provided by publisher.
Identifiers: LCCN 2020037772 (print) | LCCN 2020037773 (ebook) |
ISBN 9781515882541 (hardcover) | ISBN 9781515883630 (paperback) |
ISBN 9781515892113 (pdf)
Subjects: CYAC: Monkeys—Fiction. | Superheroes—Fiction.
Classification: LCC PZ7.K8385 Met 2021 (print) |
LCC PZ7.K8385 (ebook) | DDC [E]—dc23
LC record available at https://lccn.loc.gov/2020037772
LC ebook record available at https://lccn.loc.gov/2020037773

Designed by Ted Williams
Design Elements by Shutterstock/SilverCircle

TABLE OF CONTENTS

He came from the planet Krypton.
He is super-strong. He can fly.
He is Superman's loyal companion.
These are . . .

THE AMAZING
ADVENTURES OF

Beppo the
Super-Monkey!

CHAPTER 1

An Unusual Pearl

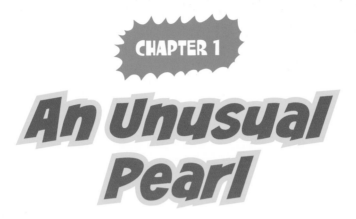

It's a quiet night. Clark Kent and

Lois Lane are dining in a seafood

restaurant. Nobody knows that Clark

is really Superman—the world's most

powerful hero.

A man sitting near them lets out

a yell of excitement.

"There's a pearl in my oyster!"

he shouts. "And it's a *red* pearl!"

Clark starts to feel tingly. He realizes

the pearl inside the man's oyster is

really a small chunk of red Kryptonite.

It affects Superman in strange ways.

The hero quickly steps outside. When

no one is looking, he changes into his

Superman suit.

Suddenly, Superman starts to shrink.

His hands get hairy. He grows a tail.

He has turned into a monkey!

"Eep! Eep! Eep!" he says.

Superman starts acting like a real

monkey too. He decides to have some

fun in the streets of Metropolis.

Superman may look like monkey, but he still has his superpowers. He picks up an empty car. He spins it like a top.

Several nearby people run away in panic.

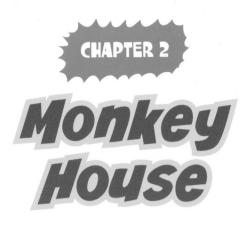

CHAPTER 2

Monkey House

In a nearby park, Beppo the Super-Monkey is relaxing on top of a tree. He is happily munching on a chocolate-covered banana.

Beppo hears people screaming. He zooms over to see what is happening.

Beppo sees the other superpowered monkey run into the Metropolis Zoo. It rips open the metal door of the monkey house exhibit.

Dozens of monkeys run through the streets of Metropolis.

Beppo flies into action. He rounds up the monkeys. He uses his heat vision to fix the door to the monkey house.

Just then, the red Kryptonite changes Superman from a regular-sized monkey into a giant gorilla! He is as tall as a two-story building!

CRASH!

The gorilla pulls a fire hydrant out of the ground. Water starts spraying everywhere!

Beppo grabs a manhole cover from the street. He uses his super-strength to slam it on top of the broken hydrant. That stops the water.

Now the gorilla is trying to lift a building. Beppo knows that he has to get the gorilla away from the city.

Beppo has an idea. He flies to the Metropolis fruit warehouse. There are giant fruits and vegetables made of plastic on the roof of the warehouse. Beppo grabs a large banana.

The gorilla licks his chops when he
sees the banana. He reaches for it.

Beppo lures him to an empty lot at
the edge of town.

CHAPTER 3

Monkey See, Monkey Do

Beppo starts digging. He creates a

deep tunnel underground.

"Monkey see, monkey do?" Beppo

asks the gorilla.

The gorilla smiles and digs. He makes

a tunnel that connects to Beppo's.

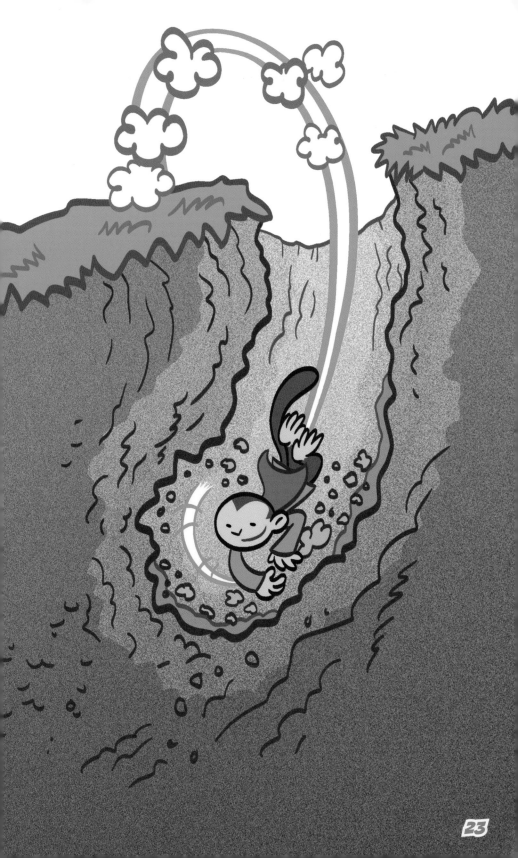

Beppo dives into his end

of the tunnel. The gorilla

copies him.

Beppo and the gorilla fly straight

toward each other as fast as they can.

There is a huge crash. The gorilla is

knocked out cold.

Beppo carries the sleeping gorilla back to the surface. A few minutes later, the red Kryptonite wears off. The gorilla turns back into Superman.

Except for a giant headache, the Man of Steel is back to normal.

"Beppo, that was quick thinking," says Superman. "You are the smartest Super-Monkey ever!"

AUTHOR!

Steve Korté is the author of many books for children and young adults. He worked at DC Comics for many years, editing more than 600 books about Superman, Batman, Wonder Woman, and the other heroes and villains in the DC Universe. He lives in New York City with his husband, Bill, and their super-cat, Duke.

ILLUSTRATOR!

Famous cartoonist Art Baltazar is the creative force behind *The New York Times* bestselling, Eisner Award-winning DC Comics' Tiny Titans; co-writer for Billy Batson and the Magic of Shazam, Young Justice, Green Lantern Animated (Comic); and artist/co-writer for the awesome Tiny Titans/Little Archie crossover, Superman Family Adventures, Super Powers, and Itty Bitty Hellboy! Art is one of the founders of Aw Yeah Comics comic shop and the ongoing comic series! Aw yeah, living the dream! He stays home and draws comics and never has to leave the house! He lives with his lovely wife, Rose, sons Sonny and Gordon, and daughter, Audrey! AW YEAH MAN! Visit him at www.artbaltazar.com

"Word Power"

exhibit (ig-ZIB-it)—a group of things or animals put out for people to see and learn about

lure (LOOR)—to cause a person to go somewhere by promising to give them something they want

manhole (MAN-hohl)—a covered hole in a street that a person can pass through to do work underneath the street

oyster (OY-stuhr)—a type of shellfish that is eaten raw or cooked

pearl (PURL)—a hard, round, shiny object made inside an oyster; pearls are used in jewelry and can be worth money

shrink (SHRINGK)—to become smaller

warehouse (WAIR-hows)—a large building used for storing or sending goods

WRITING PROMPTS

1. What if the story was told from Superman's point of view? Write a chapter of the story from the giant gorilla's perspective.

2. What do you think Lois Lane thought when Clark left? Rewrite the story with her as the main character.

3. Make a "Wanted" poster for the gorilla. How would you describe the gorilla? Add a picture.

DISCUSSION QUESTIONS

1. Think of a time someone has copied you. Why did they do it?

2. Why do you think it was important that Beppo lead the giant gorilla out of Metropolis?

3. Have you ever found anything unexpected? What was it?

Harris County Public Library, Houston, TX

THE AMAZING ADVENTURES OF THE DC SUPER-PETS!

Collect them all!